SULPHURGEDDON

IGOR RENKLAUF

Matador
Unit E2 Airfield Business Park,
Harrison Road, Market Harborough,
Leicestershire. LE16 7UL
Tel: 0116 2792299
Email: books@troubador.co.uk
Web: www.troubador.co.uk/matador
Twitter: @matadorbooks

ISBN 978 1803131 078

British Library Cataloguing in Publication Data.
A catalogue record for this book is available from the British Library.

Printed and bound in Great Britain by 4edge Limited
Typeset in 11pt Adobe Garamond Pro by Troubador Publishing Ltd, Leicester, UK

Matador is an imprint of Troubador Publishing Ltd

To all the living on this, our one and only planet

Igor Renblauf

@gmail.com

NEAR-DEATH EXPERIENCE

"I can't breathe," Mary gasped as the tightness of her chest refused to allow a new exchange of that familiar, breathful of gases past her throat.

Isaac hovered concernedly over Mary, wondering what on earth was wrong. It was quite obvious that she was having difficulty breathing; desperately, he searched for a reason, especially as they had been together in the same house all evening, and although, admittedly, the air was not as fresh as a few months ago, he had not noticed anything particular that evening. *What was it the Victorian children inhaled with a towel over their head?* Isaac wondered at a picture of an old hovel from the industrial revolution, with its attendant polluting wisps of smoke drifting across; even more worryingly, a brand-new coffin with large, round brass hinges and handles floated above the hovel, seemingly driven by a benign superforce. Another desperate coughing fit broke Isaac's reverie as Mary found great difficulty letting the air out of her lungs, which by now were full of phlegm.

John, their son, hovering in the background, suggested that lemon verbena, which might have helped his asthma in the past, would be worth a try.

Isaac tried hitting Mary's back with limited success – one moment too hard, the next too softly.

Isaac agreed to the suggestion: set to boiling the kettle to make an infusion.

The hot, calming steam eased Mary's breathing and helped her to cough the thick, sticky phlegm up out of her lungs.

With the agreement of all, and with the expectation of at least doing something to help Mary, Isaac and John decided there was no way out but to ring 999 for assistance.

They went through the standard steps with ambulance control, who suggested that a doctor should come straight away.

Mary continued to have difficulty breathing because her lungs were filling with sticky phlegm, effectively denying the gas exchange so vital to life.

No doctor arrived through the night, so by dawn, Isaac felt it would be best to take Mary to hospital himself.

Mary quickly went up through the medical hierarchy and they soon discovered a very high blood pressure of 210 over 104.

This prompted them to suspect a heart attack, treating her with calming spray on her tongue and immediately rushing her into the ambulance for transferral to the larger regional hospital.

The journey took over an hour. In that time, Mary had it explained to her that it was a heart attack.

In return, she replied that she had been poisoned by unknown fumes coming in through the vents in their bedroom in the middle of the night. She explained to the ambulance crew that it was not a heart attack but a burn in her chest. She felt burnt in her left chest; also, when she coughed up the sticky phlegm it burnt her throat too. On arrival at the big hospital, Mary was ushered to a private screened area. For some time, while waiting, white coats appeared at random from any direction. Eventually, they formed into a large group at the end of her bed.

The group of white coats listened sympathetically as she explained the timeline in-between bouts of coughing.

The interrogation really started probing into Mary's health, especially as she had mentioned the word 'poison'!

Sensory tabs were attached, printouts taken and Mary was left to wonder what the burning sensation was in her chest.

In spite of the coughing subsiding and numerous cups of tea, the time seemed to stretch towards eternity when, at 1pm, a smarter white coat popped round the corner, on his way to some other problem.

"Nothing wrong here; we can't find anything at all. You can go home now."

THE CAR

After last week's diversion to the local hospital, Isaac – not being particularly romantic, more because he felt fed up – suggested that Mary should spend a weekend away at a cheap hotel.

Mary agreed with alacrity. She, too, felt fed up. That weekend soon arrived.

Isaac had pre-packed the car in anticipation in the middle of the week. All the farm jobs were completed; John would hold the fort.

They opened the car doors in unison. As Mary sat down, she let out a shriek. "The fumes are in here too! I can't breathe again."

She coughed, spluttered and felt slightly dizzy, just like last week.

Isaac, aware he had already paid for two nights, thought it would be too short notice to cancel and claim a refund. "Well, perhaps you will feel better if we head off to begin our short break," was the best stroke of sympathy he could manage as he turned onto the main road towards the coast.

The journey to the hotel was in complete silence. They were both racking their brains as to why the car was full of the agent, probably the same agent that had sent Mary to hospital last week. What was the agent?

During the check-in process, Mary continued to complain of feeling unwell. Isaac, in an unsuccessful attempt to cheer her up, remarked at the sight of the menu for he felt hungry. Mary, feeling dizzier now after the journey, had no appetite at all. The two of them settled into their room, Isaac feeling hungrier, Mary feeling worse.

Isaac thought to himself that if they went directly to hospital early in the evening, they could run diagnostic tests to discover the cause of the distress that had been so elusive last week. After half an hour of mindless telly on the wall, Isaac's stomach came to decision time. How bad is Mary really? He offered to take her to the local cottage hospital. The good news was she was not worse, but if they could find out the cause now, it would be better than twelve hours later. Mary accepted the offer.

The white coats were in abundance, it being an early, quiet time. They hooked Mary up to various bleeping machines displaying soothing green lights. Mary was feeling better, although still noticing the familiar burning feeling to the top of her left lung. Isaac, as before, waited whilst this was X-rayed. Seated in an uncomfortable hard chair at the side of a long corridor, his mind wandered, retracing the events of the last week.

Three or four days ago, he remembered that the local lagoon had been stirred all day, giving off acrid fumes. The car had not been moved since.

Could the fumes have been trapped inside the car, then been released when Mary opened her door?

What were the fumes?

Could they be tested scientifically in a laboratory?

How could he collect fumes?

He resolved to ask Mary after the X-ray; assuming all would be well, Isaac's musing continued…

Mary appeared, looking well and smiling. "They, too, can't find anything wrong at all, so again, we are free to go home."

THE LAGOON

Arriving back at the hotel in the early hours of the following day, Isaac and Mary were certainly 'free to go home'. Isaac was annoyed, having paid for another night away, and Mary cautioned that she might be poisoned again at home by that unknown agent. Isaac had already sent an official letter to the Direktor of the Authoritorium, demanding that they investigate to determine the origin and nature of the agent. They should ascertain whether it may be linked to the lagoon; after all, the lagoon had been stirred, emitting those peppery, sickly fumes recently.

As they drove home, they discussed the probability of chemicals escaping from the lagoon half a mile away from the house. The Authoritorium was adamant that the crust on top of the lagoon was airtight and that nothing could escape, as if it was wrapped up in a blanket. Isaac was not convinced. He knew that some gases could latch on to other gases and actually lift themselves out of the soup altogether. Then he thought through the idea that when the soup had been stirred, there was no crust on top. The crust had been incorporated into the body of the soup so that it could not block the pipework during spreading. The liquid from underneath was on the surface, freely exposed to the air. That said, Mary complained that the big forager chopped up and blew the grass into trailers ready to be delivered to the concrete abomasum to make the black soup. This soup was used as fertiliser to make the next crop grow quicker and thicker, 'rocket fuel', as some would have it. She could sense that same smell that came from the stirring of the lagoon. Mary sympathised how lizards felt, sticking her tongue out to sense the flavour of the air. Her tongue was also alerted to the flavour of the ploughing and cultivating of the fields, similar to that of the stirring of the lagoon.

COLLECTION

Arriving home, Mary was very anxious, not wanting to expose herself to yet more fumes, rendering her unable to breathe again. Isaac and Mary decided they would have to escape from their house temporarily; stay with their older daughter Sophie in her big house in Deltashire.

Isaac guessed that the Authoritorium was not going to test the air for chemicals, so he decided to collect the air for testing himself.

How was he to scoop up the air?

Should he put it in a balloon somehow and take it to a laboratory?

Surely to have a decent amount of material for reagents to form the test, he would have to fill the car with balloons!

Back at the house, John reported that all was well. He had herded the cows back from the bottom fields where they had broken through the fence to seek refuge from the gadfly. There had been no lambs born. Mary started the packing ready to escape to the elder daughter's. Isaac explained to John about filling the car with balloons to take to the laboratory.

However, John had noticed that the dehumidifier seemed

to take cooking smells out of the kitchen very effectively. Not only that, but also the water to be thrown away actually smelt of the dirty oven that had yet to be cleaned.

Would that not be an effective means of gathering the chemicals ready for the lab, in the water, having been frozen out from the air?

CHEMICALS

Isaac was troubled. He understood that Mary was unable to breathe seemingly whenever the lagoon was stirred. There was a chance that chemicals could be coming off the lagoon. Apart from the acrid, peppery, burning smell of slightly rotting dead meat and veg, there were only 'sick' overtones that he could specifically recognise.

Isaac had spent the whole afternoon closer to the lagoon, moving the electric fence for the sheep. Admittedly, it had been sunny, with a brisk wind, but his face was sore, flushed and ruddy. That evening, it was flaky as if it had been dried out, lacking moisturising cream. The tubes inside his nose, that clever self-cleaning, self-lubricating filter, were blocked with sticky mucous, forcing him to breathe through his open mouth. At one stage, halfway through unreeling the fence, he felt distinctly dizzy. Yet, he felt secure in his footing, even though the ground itself seemed to be rushing up to take his place.

He again thought of the Direktor of the local Authoritorium. Surely, he would come back to him with an explanation of what was in the lagoon. After all, he had all his well-qualified staff engaged in the problem, poring over the evidence.

Later, at teatime, he opened the post to find the Direktor's reply that they had looked at everything and found there was nothing. There was no need to ask any further questions because, from now on, he was not going to respond. After this disappointing news, Isaac walked over the fields, checking the sheep. He was shocked looking at the thistles because they were wilting as if they had been sprayed with the hormone weedkiller MCPA (2-methyl-4-chlorophenoxyacetic acid) which he had used previously on another farm. As he was walking round, he noticed mouse-eared chickweed seemed to be suffering the same similar symptoms.

What else? he thought. *Maybe the wide diurnal temperature gap in the spring gave the frost an extra chill?*

That reminded him that it was spring, lambing time. So how come? John had blamed the gadfly for the determined escape of the cows to the other end of the farm. The flies fly in the summer, surely?

Certainly not in these times when the nights could be so cold that the snow shower could rest on the ground undisturbed for the morning, till the sun bathed the ground in warmth and light. Mary, appreciating the normal sparkles of the snow, examined it in the light of the sun with her hand lens and noticed in amongst the blanket that there were some minute sparkles that shone more and looked whiter than the rest. Mary took her phone from her pocket, snapped the snow for prosperity. On inspection of the photo, the white sparkles had been intensified, brighter and whiter than white.

Then John thought of the balloons in the car.

John's idea of freezing chemicals out of the air with the dehumidifier was a much better way of concentrating the unknown gas into one place, ready for testing.

As Isaac checked the animals in the barn, he was sad to see poor old Wheezer, a fifteen-month steer, labouredly wheezing for breath with copious phlegm drooling from his mouth. He must have had a hit of fumes over the last few days. Isaac was weighing up the decision whether Wheezer would have to move on if he was not going to get any better.

Now, Isaac was more troubled.

FIDO THE FAITHFUL

Fido, the faithful came from a long line of pedigree border collies.

He was descended from Churchill's Flash, a trialling champion from long ago. By repute, whenever Mr Churchill felt thirsty, Flash could do the earning, by doing the deed, and Mr Churchill would be paid the appropriate fee in the matching number of bottles of whisky. As Fido was already pre-programmed, his training was minimal, so he soon learnt his left and right, pushes and back offs; shedding came naturally to him. What Fido really enjoyed was hunting game and wildlife. His nose was very accurate; many a spaniel would go past the quarry without even noticing it, whereas Fido could point, then flush and retrieve the quarry back after it had been shot. Often, John or Isaac had no trouble coming home with a brace of pheasants for supper.

Isaac had seen so many oak trees – only around twenty years old, by then safely established – ruined by the ringbarking of the leader shoot by grey squirrels in the spring. It was in the spring that the sap was particularly delicious, containing essential minerals for their metabolism. Fido liked to come up behind these squirrels on the ground by surprise, so that they rushed up the trees to safety, only to be caught by the shot from John's gun.

Last autumn, Isaac and Fido had joined the beaters on a neighbour's farm, not far from the lagoon, herding the pheasants and partridges to fly over the guns. Fido covered hectares of ground, searched acres of undergrowth, thoroughly enjoying this exciting task.

After a smoky bonfire night, he developed an annoying tickle in his throat. Isaac mocked Fido about it, saying perhaps he ought to be vaccinated against kennel cough. He must have caught it off some of the other dogs. Some days he felt tired and sleepy; he was worried that his exceptional nose might not be as accurate as it used to be. Would he be able to follow and catch the runners, the pricked birds? Through the spring months, he looked forward to lambing time: mothering up the ewes and lambs so that Isaac and John could be sure that the ewes had their own lambs and all were fed satisfactorily. His nose would not be so important to him then. Even so, he still had this annoying tickle in his throat. After a while, sitting on his bed, he found himself coughing up phlegm.

Perhaps it was kennel cough, after all. Fortunately, he could rest, as he had heard that they were going away to stay with the daughter, John's big sister Sophie.

GCMS

Mary was in the midst of packing to go to Sophie's when she realised nobody had emptied the dehumidifier into the special clean bottles for the laboratory so that the water could be tested with the certain knowledge that it would be free of contaminants.

Isaac thought back. He remembered that you could find how much of a chemical was in a solution by using a laboratory procedure of dropping measured amounts of specific reagents into that solution with a burette until the colour changed. At that point, there was a simple calculation involving 'moles' (he had never understood them) that would give the desired answer. That assumed that the chemistry of the solution was known.

Isaac challenged Mary – how was the lab going to find out the chemistry of the solution?

Mary was not fazed by this antagonistically posed question. She had explained the problem to the lab, which operated the modern, state-of-the-art equipment. They recommended an organic multi-screen GCMS.

The sample would be heated to separate its constituents, gas chromatography (GC). Then, with mass spectrometry

(MS), the bits would be weighed to identify their form and quantity, to be printed out automatically.

Isaac was surprised to learn that to arrive at the answer, it would take at least ten days, so he was determined to take the sample to the lab straight away on the journey to Sophie's house.

Isaac also wondered whether the chemical smells were more prevalent in the evenings and at night. It was then that the temperature inversion occurred when the leftover warm air of the daytime blanketed the smells close to the ground. By contrast, the warm, sunny days allowed the smells to rise up with the pollutants high above ground level, therefore not being so noticeable. In which case, the air smelt fresher.

AWAY FROM THE FARM

On arrival at Sophie's house, Mary was still feeling weak, not willing or ready to talk about the latest sequence of events and how they had commissioned GCMS tests to Sophie's husband Fredrick, a larger-than-life businessman.

The next day, with Mary feeling slightly better, Fredrick was ready to play devil's advocate. Fredrick's main plank of good sense was that Mary must eliminate all the other things that might be causing her distressing symptoms. For instance, how could the smoke coming from the wood burner be eliminated? That was just what the local Authoritorium had suggested with their latest letter to fend off suggestions to put a 'statutory nuisance' on the lagoon. They were, after all, the authority with binding statutory legal status. Unlike the 'Authoritorium of Health', who were only there in an advisory capacity which must be sought to solve a problem of an Authoritarian, be it local or central.

Mary, though slightly better, was still coughing sticky, stinging phlegm, feeling shivery inside and sick all the time, in spite of being in the fresher air of Deltashire.

Fredrick was ready to press home his contribution, especially as his morning was free of appointments. Being a keen businessman, he had a deep understanding of human nastiness. He was always ready to turn the tables, especially on the Authoritorium, who had not served him well in the past. As Isaac said, "Half the world wants to create something; the other half wants to prevent the former from achieving it."

Isaac had explained about the weeds looking as if they had been sprayed with MCPA (2-methyl-4-chlorophenoxyacetic acid), a spray that he had used on several farms before against nettles, docks, dandelions, daisies and soft rushes. In Isaac's experience, the MCPA seemed to encourage the weed growth the following year when the thistles seemed to grow thicker than ever.

This may have been an example of homeopatheticism, in which Fredrick did not believe. Fredrick was sceptical about the thistles suffering; after all, they were 'injurious weeds', so what was he worrying about? However, Isaac, not listening, started on about the poor cow wheat not looking healthy. These plants had gone black a few days after the black soup had been spread next door.

Fredrick reverted back to his main line of argument. "You must establish 'source – pathway – destination'. Quoting the fact there is a lagoon in the countryside is only the first of three steps. As for looking at MCPA, it is sprayed everywhere; farmers improve their grassland for more yield and therefore more money."

With which, they went back to Sophie to discuss their return to imminent lambing back at the farm. Sophie, having listened to the discussions with Fredrick, wanted to say her pennyworth before they left. She was suffering from a sore throat and at times felt extremely thirsty. The air was not so fresh as in former times. Mary retorted that Isaac was much grumpier these days, possibly too much stale air or maybe he, too, was smelling the mystery fumes of burning dog 'poo' in plastic bags mixed with vomit that they had seen reported in the newspapers around the country.

The ewes would wait no longer.

LEAF TESTS

Fredrick was disappointed not to have made more progress with Mary and Isaac; between them all, they were stuck on the phenoxyacetic acid. Mary and Isaac felt the same disappointment on their return home to the farm. All Fredrick could repeat was 'source – pathway – destination'.

Back at the farm, there was another worry. The camellia bushes that had been planted three weeks ago, originally bursting with promise and in the peak of health, were now looking sick, with strangely coloured orange leaves. John had taken samples to the local nursery, where one of the girls had looked after camellias on her university course. She examined them carefully. Certainly, for her, the leaves were a bright orange colour that she had not seen before. Also, some of the leaves were brown and dead at their ends. Although she had had the usual spring frost that year, the other plants in the nursery had not suffered unduly.

John returned to the lambing.

On his way, he passed by poor old Wheezer, who was drooling, breathing no better and in fact, he looked thinner.

John rang the kennels.

Poor old Wheezer was gone on.

It was something to do with his lungs and breathing, as if he was suffering from lungworm.

"Did you not ring the vet, then?" Mary, back from Sophie's, challenged at teatime.

Isaac and John replied in unison, "What, and get yet another bill!"

While they were catching up at teatime, the subject of the sickly camellias was discussed. Isaac thought he had seen Glen (the next-door farmer) out with his sprayer. Glen was a very tidy farmer and liked to see everything looking very productive. John thought he had better ask if Glen was up to date with the spraying, whether he had done enough this year; the reply came that they had. Glen, a concerned, sympathetic neighbour, offered John a leaflet on the spray, Starane. Isaac had used this chemical on his farm years ago to rid the wheat and barley of cleavers, or 'erif', as they called it locally. Starane is the trade name of fluroxypyr 1-methylheptyl ester (MHE) which is [(4-Amino-3,5-dichloro-6-fluoro-2-pyridinyl)oxy] acetic acid.

Starane mimics the auxins, e.g. indole-3-acetic acid, as does MCPA, similar to 2,4-D being half of Agent Orange. 2,4,5-T makes the rest of that agent.

Therefore, Isaac thought the orange colour of the leaves could be related to Agent Orange.

Rather than stay in a mist of Agent Orange all night, Mary preferred to go to the local town to stay with her friend Lady Penelope.

LAMBING TIME

Prima Luce, the phrase that Caesar used to start his chapters in his diaries *De Bello Gallico* of his travels conquering Europe, translates as 'at first light'. Like Caesar, Isaac and Fido appreciated that time of the day in the spring when the mothering up of the ewes and lambs was the most efficient. It is then that the humidity of the air is still high, the sun has yet to move the scent off the ground and the ewes are better able to check for their own lambs by smell. Isaac always pondered whether they told them apart because either they smelt right or they did not smell wrong. Which? Anyway, the ewes and lambs were ready for breakfast as the flock mobilised for grazing, expecting to tackle another day. Fido would push all the lambs in the field to one corner, then Isaac would allow the individual ewes with their own lambs to make a controlled escape back into the middle of the field. Fido was ready to chase round to cover anybody who was obviously not part of the family that Isaac was allowing. Fido thoroughly enjoyed this challenge, whatever the weather; quite often in the spring it could be very wet – Fido would be plastered in mud. Isaac, aware that Mary was complaining about the dusty shelves in

Fido's lobby back at the farmhouse, made sure to throw Fido into the pond to wash the mud off before they went home for breakfast themselves.

Over breakfast, they discussed the problems in the lambing shed. John had been trying to lamb a ewe; the lamb's head was stuck. As always, the first task was to identify how the lamb(s) were presenting. A task easier said than done. However, years of experience usually catered for all normal cases. In this case, everything was presenting normally, except that the first lamb would not come out and seemed to be stuck within the ewe's womb. Isaac was sure that the lamb was not coming out far enough, so they had to consider the options.

A. Call the vet – yet another expensive bill, with an unknown outcome.
B. Shoot the ewe – hope to get live lambs immediately after the ewe has died.
C. Wait to see if she makes progress on her own – lose dead lambs or save ewe maybe?
D. On further reflection: caesar her quickly as she is nicely opened up, her bone ligaments are fully relaxed ready for lambing; now being the time to go back to B.

Isaac weighed up the situation, bearing in mind that the ewe was not in the first flush of youth, thinking that the large size of the lambs may be causing the problem, or even Siamese twins, as John was saying. So, he reluctantly decided that the lambs were more important than their mother, who sadly by now was not worth so much money. Mary, aware of most decisions on the farm, at this point readied herself in preparation. They continued with plan B. Mary wielded the scalpel to release two large lambs. They soon confirmed why the lamb was stuck – he was welded to his twin brother. They were in fact Siamese twins joined at the hip. Isaac remembered, just after Chernobyl, the double lamb joined all the way down so that he had eight legs, four ears and two heads, one of which had a large Cyclops eye in the middle of his forehead. Isaac had always blamed the radiation from the mushroom cloud from the original explosion in Russia that was blown over towards Wales. Whatever, the textbooks would claim these as congenital deformities and probably not mention the high dose of radiation and its crippling effect on living creatures.

SMELL SHEETS

After continued complaints about the fumes from the lagoon spreading in the air on the wind, the Direktor of the Authoritorium dispatched one of his operatives to talk to Mary, who was continuing to suffer from fumes back at the farm. The operative made a timed appointment to check for the fumes back at the house. At the appointed hour, no one was to be seen. However, just before Mary and Isaac decided to leave, thinking they had been stood up, the operative breezed in with the glib excuse that he had been checking the neighbour's property too, having seen that their light was on. Mary started grumbling about the time and the appointment, to which the operative cautioned her that he was there to help and that he could just as soon go away for his tea, for which he was now very late. Although he had his 'sniffer's certificate', he found no smells emanating from inside the dishwasher, which had remained full of unwashed dishes and unopened for the last month. His next observation was the state of the chimney and whether it had recently been swept. Isaac started to broach the subject of the MCPA/Agent Orange chemicals, only to find that the operative's chemical knowledge was limited to sampling the drinking water from home supplies, the testing for which was done far away 'up north'. Isaac explained how the local rocks provided water of pH 7, the perfect neutrality for the alimentary canal and copper pipework. The operative changed the subject and went on to repeat how his tea would be getting cold. In a gloating tone, he would be back to test the water from the spring, Isaac's home supply. The Authoritorium had the right to close the supply down for the common good even though the thirst-quenching spring fed only one family. Isaac was worried. The operative, just before he left, gave him a 'smell sheet' to be filled in whenever anyone was affected.

THE CAMELLIAS

The Authoritorium's 'smell sheet' acted like a sop to its consciousness. Certainly, when read by anyone, the fume problem was recognised and verified, for instance to the Direktor. Mary and Lady Penelope asked themselves if anyone else would see their damning sheet. Lady Penelope had come to the farm to help Mary in the vegetable garden and weeding the camellia plants. The grass had outgrown the camellias that were now hidden in the undergrowth. The camellia leaves that were exposed still had that strange orange colour, whereas underneath, they were a luxuriant green. That scenario could be explained by the spray drift that John had discovered from next door. Mary and Lady Penelope asked themselves if they would do better to allow the camellias to hide in the undergrowth.

Later, Mary opened the post to find the results from the laboratory. She showed and discussed them with Lady Penelope. These results showed that the phenoxyacetic acid was prominent. After speaking to one of the operatives of the Authoritorium, Mary was persuaded that this substance was a common additive to foods in the food manufacturing industry. Isaac was not convinced but wanted to take more notice of the concentrations which he thought were low. Bear in mind that these were of gases frozen from the air that they all breathed normally.

Yet to Mary and Lady Penelope, it was a revelation that they were breathing in phenolic compounds, and further down the list were several different creosols. Isaac added the concentrations of each chemical and found that the phenolics lumped together were above the working eight-hour day limit for exposure. On the way back to Lady Penelope's past the lagoon, Lady Penelope and Isaac lost their voices. They could only speak in a croaky whisper. Mary likened them to the dawn chorus which, although it was the right time of the year, had been noticeably absent this time. Isaac croaked that he had hardly heard the birds this lambing time and it reminded him of *Silent Spring* by Rachel Carson.

The next morning, they were listening for the feeble dawn chorus now that it had been flagged up, but that usual cacophony was missing. Perhaps the birds had gone croaky too and could not sing properly. Isaac thought he was too old, nearly seventy, for his voice to be breaking naturally, again.

Lady Penelope, after Isaac and Mary had returned to the farm for more lambing, was keen to do her handwashing so that she could keep up to date. Halfway through, before even rinsing the clothes out, the tips of her fingers grew painful blisters, as if she had tried to touch-type on a hot plate as the keys. Yesterday, she had worked hard weeding. *But surely not so hard as to deserve this*, she thought.

CASE LAW

Poor Lady Penelope, her fingers could no longer work the word processor.

Fortunately, her brain was still active so she continued to process the words in a legal fashion. She was well aware of the English legal system that relied on case law, in contrast to the European way of making laws that did not always fit the bill and were not relevant to every case. She started to explain to Isaac and Mary that this scenario was very similar to 'Ryland and Fletcher' which describes the nuisance of the nearby quarry leaking water onto the neighbouring property with expensive consequences. Among the many defences, if the statutory authority, the Authoritorium, approves or does not resist the accumulation of a thing, in this case the 'stench', then the Ryland and Fletcher scenario would be invalidated and there would be no case to answer. The Authoritorium had already stated that the 'stench' could not travel more than 200m. Mary chirped up to say that her friends, the lichenologists, had surveyed the local woodland previously. Their studies came to the conclusion that the change in prevalence of species must be due to some form of chemical attack. Lady Penelope was unsure, though she knew that the different lichen populations were also used to measure severity of local air pollution. Isaac, listening to this discussion, was convinced that they had to find the offending chemical.

He collected a large sample of leaves from the damaged camellias, expecting after talking to the laboratory that the Starane – the chemical agent, as he was convinced – would be found and be able to be quantified. Then, there might be a legal case.

THE DOWSER

Mary was religiously filling in the 'smell sheets', trying to explain how the air was peppery, smelt like hot burnt toast or rubber and sometimes like dead, burning meat. The air irritated her nose and made her chest feel burnt at the top left. Her heartbeat was rubbery and unreliable. Some of the Authoritorium operatives had suggested that Mary's problems were purely psychosomatic. This accusation did not please Mary at all. Basically, she thought that they were accusing her of making it all up. Another of her friends was very knowledgeable about dowsing, not only for water, how potable it would be and its depth, but also for health problems and other abstract subjects. Mary decided to go for a test to find out what was causing her distressing symptoms. The dowser asked a few questions, for instance, what was bothering her. They sat together quietly. In front of him he had a list of annoying chemicals over which he pointed; in the other hand he asked his pendulum. The list included weedkillers, paints, cleaning fluids, which the pendulum ignored as it constantly settled on SO_2. After several confirmatory runs through the lists, there was no doubt – it was this sulphur compound, to the surprise, and somewhat dismay, of Isaac, who was certain that phenoxyacetic acid, allied to the weedkillers, was the cause of the problem.

The Authoritorium's operative poured scorn on the suggestion that sulphur dioxide was the offending chemical because nothing had been burnt.

MYSTERY FOAM

Mary was visiting Sophie so she would not be back until the evening. Isaac spent all the morning cogitating, so much so he left the water on, returning to a flood of all the lamb pens. The little lambs did not appreciate their wet bed, having to stand up on their little feet out of the flood. So, he now had to clean all the pens up, ready for the evening.

Sure enough, Mary returned in the early evening, full of news from Sophie's. Mary was explaining how Sophie's village was full of chemical smells from their local lagoon, making Sophie feel she had a constant cold, was continuously thirsty, as well as having an itchy spot of skin on her back. Some plants in Sophie's garden had that same orange colouring, identical to the plants, especially the beech leaves on the lane to the lagoon at home. At the bottom of Sophie's garden was a hedge separating the curtilage of the house from her field, around which grew some majestic old oak trees. The leaves at the tops of the crowns seemed very sparse, small, dry, crinkly and discoloured. Rather than the usual dark British racing green, the leaves showed a sickly pale lime green with occasional small brown spots. At the bottom of the field, there ran a small brook of clear water where the dipper lived. In the eddies of the current where it ran slowly, great lumps of foam rested, unable to follow the main flow downstream. Mary picked up some foam for examination. Surprisingly, inside the nest of bubbles were a few motionless flies and invertebrates. In fact, it all looked pretty lifeless, yet the water was clear and the basic tests for agricultural pollution, ammonia and phosphates were showing low levels. The water did not smell. Mary dried a drop of the stream water on a glass slide to reveal an opaque film of minute white particles.

EPICORMICS

Isaac was researching the Authoritorium's response, saying that there was no reason for there to be any SO_2 around because there had been no burning.

Certainly, Mary's symptoms – her inability to breathe, her wheeziness – were all factors that pointed back to the Great Smog of 1952. Then, the victims were labelled as respiratory cripples because they just could not function at all, no air. Just after the Second World War, the country – through a cold spell in December – was burning much poor-quality coal, producing smoke that normally contained SO_2, which with water and oxygen turned into SO_3, thence into sulphuric acid. It is more likely that it was the sulphuric acid that burnt the victims' lungs. Isaac had to admit that he could see the similarities of the 1952 smog to Mary's symptoms.

Not only that, but Mary's lichenologist friends had remarked on the profuse epicormic growth on a row of oak trees growing in a relict hedge by a spring in a nearby field. Actually, looking up at the canopies, they were very thin and the grass underneath the trees was growing well. Usually, the shadow from the canopy would be enough to make the grass grow thin and poor; under very large trees the shadow was dark enough to kill the grass altogether. Isaac remembered that the canopy should send enough hormone down the trunk to silence the epicormic buds, but now these buds were being encouraged to shoot by the extra light from the feeble canopy and by there being no hormone to stop them growing. The lichenologists also remarked that the lichens had changed type to the high-pollution species. The new leaves of the oaks were far smaller than usual, coloured red, orange and yellow, more like in autumn.

While Isaac was following the Authoritorium's response, he could not find any answers to the 'smell sheets'. When he started to fill them in, he had thought that the Authoritorium's conscience would be sated at the recognition of these problems occurring locally. So, he rang them up; they suggested that any comments Mary and Isaac had should be put on an emergency dedicated email, which could be looked at by the operatives in real time so that they could 'action' accordingly.

WEEDKILLER RESULTS

Isaac was hungry for a late breakfast, having mothered up all the ewes and lambs with Fido. All around the farm, he kept noticing different plants with the tell-tale signs of spray drift of hormone killers like MCPA. For instance, the mouse-eared chickweed had turned brown; the docks had brown dots on their leaves. The new brambles had a bright red colour to their leaves instead of normal green.

It was cold that morning, just after *prima luce*; when Fido and Isaac started, there was a white frost over the fields, through which the sheep had made green tracks as soon as they stirred to go foraging.

Isaac started to open the post back at the farmhouse but was interrupted by Fido who, with his kennel cough, was voiding the morning's phlegm from running around the fields. Mary sympathised with Fido and his heap of phlegm. "I know how you feel," she said, as she too had been coughing up phlegm all night.

Isaac opened the laboratory results of the leaves to find the concentration of MCPA had come back as less than 10 ug/L. On the phone, the technician said he was sorry that there was no weedkiller in the leaves. Isaac challenged him, saying that there must have been some chemical even though the concentration was less than 10 ug/L. The technician explained further that there were various levels that could be reported from the tests. The lowest was zero – that being no trace of the chemical – then there was the limit of detection; then there was the limit of quantification, able to provide accurate levels; then there was a level of legal significance which the Authoritorium would use. This sample was above zero but below the limit of detection.

Legally, it would be counted as zero.

Now he had lost his appetite for breakfast.

PASS THE PARCEL

Isaac still could not believe that the camellia leaves were not suffering from the weedkiller drift from the neighbour. He searched the chemical list from the dehumidifier; it included creosols, phenols, triphenyl phosphate, pyridine and many more, some of which were present at levels above the eight-hour cumulative exposure limit for the workplace.

He searched the smell status forms sent to the Authoritorium for any other clues. What was the cause of her distressing symptoms: stinging tongue, coughing, stomach aches, odd sores, brain confusion?

Mary disturbed Isaac's investigation by saying they would have to look somewhere else. For instance, the local lagoon; many of the problems seemed to be pointing in that direction.

Now that Mary was reporting directly to the Authoritorium and the various associated organisations, she was finding their responses at best annoying and at worst nasty. For instance, she would start by contacting the Authoritorium of Health, who would say 'poor you', and in case this was medical, she should go to the public health page to cover their backs. That page would say, 'Go to Accident and Emergency', who would tell

Mary to go to her own doctor, who would then be surprised that the local Authoritorium had done no tests. The Authoritorium, who had done, was the comprehensive central government Authoritorium who denied any liability because they did not issue any licences, so it was nothing to do with them. Perhaps she should go to the local fire service, who suggested going to the local Authoritorium. The doctor then also suggested the local Authoritorium, who replied, "Perhaps go to the Public Health Authoritorium who are good at statistics, and they should liaise with Health and Safety." They then came to the conclusion that there had been failure in the regulatory procedure.

As for nastiness, the local Authoritorium started to explain how Mary's symptoms must be psychosomatic, meaning that she did not suffer anything and therefore it must all be made up in her mind.

Isaac likened this attitude to the treatment of the witches in the Middle Ages, trial by ordeal, a simple test whereby the victims – the witches – were tied up, then thrown into the river; those who sank would be deemed innocent. Those who managed to escape by reaching the shore would be guilty and therefore have to await further attention from the authority.

A similar ploy devised by the Authoritorium was that Mary should experience the discharge from the lagoon remotely but be unaware when exactly it was happening. If she choked, she would be deemed to be innocent.

Mary thought that to make progress they must ask another analytical chemist to investigate with different methods of chemical tests. The new tests would use special test tubes to catch the air for hydrogen sulphide and sulphur dioxide and round buttons to catch various other chemicals to be analysed later.

TRAIN TO LONDON

Mary needed a break from the lambing, so she went up to London on the train to visit her other daughter Eliza. She found that they had offered her a first-class seat at the front. The seats were very plush and comfortable. It was strange that on the journey, the air from the air conditioning tightened her throat, which triggered another coughing fit. She did not feel well. By the time she got to Paddington, walking past the engine blowing hot air, she felt sick and was pleased to breathe the cleaner, though polluted, air of London. On her return journey past Sarum Plain, Mary held a fascinating conversation with a fellow passenger, who was concerned about the effects of 5G and its unreported possible radiation effects. He said that the new masts were suddenly appearing by stealth. He had noticed that the trees surrounding them were dying and that their leaves looked burnt. Mary recognised the description of these afflicted trees. She compared them to the photos of the vegetation around the lagoon. There were marked similarities. Halfway down the train track, that same smell wafted in again, causing the neighbouring occupants around her to surreptitiously, subconsciously respond by gently clearing their throats.

Isaac welcomed Mary back at their home station. Mary explained to Isaac how lovely and fresh the air was in London, how the greenery in the parks was growing with unrestrained vigour, with leaves succulent and verdant. Isaac was surprised, having read in the *Daily Trumpet* reporting of yesterday's mystery fumes that there was a wave of the stench, battery acid mixed with disinfectant, on the outskirts of London. Nobody seemed to know of its origin.

BEAN

After mothering up, Fido and Isaac checked the small herd of cows which should have been in calf after repeated attempts by the artificial insemination man.

Although Isaac had the veterinary to check them all, there was only one, number 138, due soon. The rest, although looking fat, were not in calf. The veterinary had taken blood samples that showed they were low in vitamin B12, a classic local problem induced by cobalt deficiency in the soil. In the previous century, the roving dealers recognised this problem in the sheep and classified it as 'pine'. The sheep would be very hungry and would waste away unless they were moved to another part of the country with a different soil make-up, preferably with more cobalt. Of course, the dealer would recognise the symptoms and be able to match the appropriate soil for the poorly animals. Once the transaction was completed, the animals and the dealer would thrive.

However, number 138 was indeed showing the tell-tale pre-calving symptoms: tail up, agitation, bones relaxed, ready to calve. *Best to check after breakfast*, thought Isaac. That he did, only to find that the calf was not making progress. So, Isaac went to fetch the calving ropes. Having successfully delivered a live calf without too much difficulty, Isaac found the new calf remarkably dozy. No. 138 was enthusiastic that her beloved new arrival should be more responsive. She licked him all over, polishing his coat, biting his navel and uttering tender moos. Still, he was happy just to have arrived in the world. Isaac thought it probably best that he wait another couple of hours for him to increase his appetite before offering his head up to 138's teat. Then, he did suckle, but still without any enthusiasm; he preferred that Isaac should hold his head up, then, reluctantly he would suckle normally but slowly. The calf, now named Bean, had probably had enough colostrum which would ensure that he would have enough antibodies to stave off infections from the standard diseases common to that farm.

THE BURN

Now, three quarters of the way through the lambing, and with the added extra jobs caused by the new calf Bean, Isaac and Fido noticed a couple of lambs limping during the mothering up rounds. Isaac suspected they were victims of the dreaded joint ill. After Isaac and Fido had caught them, Isaac could feel their swollen joints. In the past, he had had a religious routine to dip all newborn lambs' navels in a bottle of iodine to stave off the E. coli infection spreading through their navels. He now explained to Mary that perhaps they should return to that policy. Mary reacted to the possibility, or even the accusation, that she had not been conscientious on that front by revealing the contents of the day's post, the results from the buttons and sulphur dioxide and hydrogen sulphide tests. The only significant result came from the buttons that had found an overexaggerated level of elemental sulphur, which the lab technicians put down to an error in the testing procedure, therefore should and could not be counted.

That evening, Isaac brought in another spare lamb from a triplet. Mary would have to give the hungry lamb a bottle of colostrum and put him in the box under the lamp to keep him warm. Mary asked Isaac whether the lamb had been given his dose of iodine, in spite of the umbilical cord being soaked in iodine. Towards the end of lambing, the temperature of the staff's mood was always raised. Isaac said nothing, but to keep the peace, he once again checked the lamb's navel. Mary settled the lamb on her lap for feeding. Her trousers were covered in iodine and lamb stink, so she decided to jump in a hot bath to clean up before supper. She had thought she would be able to relax, but the iodine mark on her leg was really painful and red as if she had been burnt there.

She had never been allergic to iodine and the bath water was hot but no hotter than usual. The large, stained mark, as big as the palm of her hand, started to blister. That night, Mary could not sleep, partly because her burnt leg hurt but also because the lamb in the box, who was well fed and warm under the lamp, was bawling with an urgent note to his voice as if he was in pain. In the morning, Mary went to feed him. He was motionless, dead. His navel was swollen, pitch-black and necrotic.

SARUM

Isaac, Fido and John quickly achieved the mothering up in the morning because Isaac and Mary had decided to take the day off to go to Sarum, which had recently received much publicity. John was to look after Bean, who at last was able to follow his mother, slowly, in the field. Sometimes, though, when it was warm and sunny, Bean would lie down exhausted, only to fall asleep; his mother 138 would soon miss him and return to allow him to suckle.

The journey to Sarum was an ideal opportunity for Mary, still aware of the itching of the healing of the large blister on her leg, gave her time to research the chemistry of hot water and iodine. It was not long into the journey that Mary discovered the Bunsen reaction: the first part of the process for extracting hydrogen from water.

$$2H_2O + SO_2 + I_2 \xrightarrow{\text{heat}} H_2SO_4 + 2HI$$

She thought back to the dowser's pendulum that had pointed to the sulphur dioxide and understood that sulphuric acid must have been the cause of her burn.

Just as they were approaching the outskirts of Sarum, a massive silver articulated tanker careered onto the main road out of a farm track. Isaac was annoyed that the tanker had been unable to slow down and give him right of way. At the rear of the tanker, there was a chimney which was emitting a faint haze.

As they followed, Isaac went croaky; once again his voice seemed to be breaking. How young was he? Mary started to cough, breathing in the haze from the chimney, that familiar cooking smell of rotting meat and vegetables reminiscent of the lagoon stirrings. As at home, her phlegm stung her tongue, which by now was sore. Mary also felt sick.

Locking up the car, Isaac could see Mary was looking at the leaves on the bank of the car park by the river, saying that they were identical to those at home, especially the burnt edges of the laurels and abnormal brightly coloured new leaves of beech and sycamore.

They walked through the town, past the squares still cordoned off, to the cathedral close. How amazing that the cathedral still had plenty of space around it. Once inside, they marvelled at the majesty of the enclosed volume and how light and airy it was for such a massive stone building. Isaac could not keep his eyes off a populated statue scene of the crucifixion procession in an alcove on the north wall. He could recognise Herod by his authoritative and thoughtful air, the centurion, clothed in military efficiency, the concerned peasant girl, who was being calmed by Jesus himself, allaying the crowd's fears and excitement along the path to the eventual final destination. On the way back to the car, they stopped for ice creams served by a girl who kept clearing her throat and complaining that she had been suffering from a cough for weeks since Christmas, in spite of daily doses of ice cream and several courses of antibiotics, none of which had had any beneficial effect.

On the way back, Isaac was keen to show Mary the view from the main road, pointing to the west, that he used to travel on the way to holidays during his childhood. They could see the bent spire of the cathedral; Isaac had always compared that to the 'Leaning Tower of Pisa'. Following on from that view, Isaac explained that the barrack huts were the site of the cold research unit, where anyone could have a free holiday at the government's expense for one or two weeks while they were investigating the common cold. Whenever they had passed there, his father had always said, "They won't find the answer to the common cold there." Now, of course, with the benefit of hindsight and science, we know that similar symptoms do not always point to the same problem or even the same cause, for example, 'dipper's flu'. Thus, after an enjoyable day out, they wended their way back to the farm, Mary determined to follow up on the iodine clue and do further research into sulphur in the air.

SULPHUR

Prima luce, Fido and Isaac mothered up the ewes and lambs again.

Isaac was perplexed that Mary was tackling the latest sulphur-iodine revelation with so much enthusiasm. He was wary that they might be going down the wrong path. He was still smarting from the hormone weedkiller, MCPA etc. setback. After the ewes and lambs, they checked Bean, who was in the same spot as last night. He seemed very stiff in his joints. Perhaps he too was suffering from joint ill. Back for breakfast, Isaac reluctantly called the vet. Mary was sorting through the post, reading through the results of the special test tubes for hydrogen sulphide and sulphur dioxide and the round buttons. She read that the results from the buttons had been discounted because of an error in the testing procedure but wondered if they might actually be true after all. The buttons were showing an abnormally high level of elemental octasulfur in the air. This idea spurred Mary on. She managed to broker a deal with another laboratory to test the water from the dehumidifier for sulphates, sulphides and sulphur, which required different laboratory procedures for each compound.

The vet arrived before they had finished breakfast. He inspected Bean, gave him some analgesics to ease the pain of walking and some antibiotics for suspected joint ill. He discussed the blood test that was pointing to cobalt deficiency that would be linked to selenium deficiency, white muscle disease, which could also explain Bean's reluctance to walk after his mother.

In the meantime, Mary continued asking the laboratory about octasulfur, finding out that it was a puckered ring of eight sulphur atoms attached together in a shape like a crown or a corona. The sulphur and carbon chemistry were a subdivision of organic and biological chemistry.

The technician explained that the pure elemental sulphur was insoluble in water, unlike sulphates and the reduced version of sulphur, H_2S, with good solubility at pH 8.

Mary then filled in the 'smell sheet', saying that her tongue was sore again, probably caused by the fissures along its length. In fact, someone had suggested to her that these fissures often occurred in 'down and outs' with a poor diet, resulting in smelly breath caused by sulphur producing bacteria in a dirty mouth.

BUBBLES

Prima luce. Fido and Isaac had to be careful crossing the road to the sheep field to avoid a stream of cars coming from a late finishing party. In one of the last cars was a talkative Melvin, from the farm next door, who was explaining that the party was celebrating the signing of new contracts. There had been plenty of champagne flowing with the release of tiny 'beaded bubbles winking at the brim'. Melvin was wondering in amazement at the longevity of the bubbles, even after the pressure lowered by a couple of atmospheres on the bubbles by the popping of corks. On account of the carbon dioxide being formed in discrete, small bubbles by yeast eating sugars from the tirage, leading to this secondary fermentation, the wine was carbonated. The bubbles were so small that they could be classed as microbubbles; as such, they would not have enough buoyancy to rise out of the champagne.

Fido and Isaac managed to cross the road, do the mothering up and proceed to Bean's field. Bean was up and about and dutifully following his mother 138, as he should have been before Isaac had called the veterinary. Isaac had to repair the mobile chicken coop that was needed for the batch of table chickens so that they had access to fresh grass all the time to improve their flavour; as an added benefit, Isaac would be able to cut down on the bought food, thus saving money.

Back for breakfast, Isaac caught up with Mary's latest campaign against the black soup, the most likely reason for her troubling symptoms, about which she and Isaac had repeatedly questioned the Direktor of the Authoritorium.

Isaac was going back over the idea that there was plenty of sulphur about from the testing. He had visions of a masked Peruvian peasant carrying blocks of sulphur on his back dug from the brim of an old volcano on the ring of fire around the Pacific. It seemed this stoic peasant was fighting the sulphurous fumes with an inadequate but colourful kerchief wrapped around his face. At least he was carrying the burden downhill, not requiring so much oxygen, the flow of which was impeded by his dirty red kerchief. Interestingly, sulphur was to be found in many places around the world, sometimes not associated with volcanoes but also with anaerobic digestion of plant life of many years ago. In fact, the vast majority of the annual sixty-four million tonnes of sulphur produced worldwide in 2005 was by-product sulphur from refineries and other hydrocarbon, fossil fuel, processing plants.

It was a late post that day; Mary found the three sulphur test results: virtually no sulphates or sulphides, but 40 mg/L elemental sulphur had been present in the hallway at home. Was this another false testing result from erroneous equipment?

BLACK SOUP

Now with the earlier dawn, at the same time as usual, Fido and Isaac crossed the road again on the way to the sheep field. Just at that moment, they encountered Melvin driving his big tanker of black soup, much recovered from his celebrations the other day. Fido, walking behind the tanker, had another bout of kennel cough. He looked very sleepy too, as if his mind was on other things. Isaac looked up at Melvin in his modern cab, with all the electronic instruments. "Don't get lost around the home fields," quipped Isaac. Around the back of the trailer, the air was full of the taste of warm cooking, mixed with sickly cabbage and burnt toast. As Melvin drove away, Isaac thought that the smell of the tanker had changed to battery acid. Isaac looked up, noticing the burnt and partially shrivelled look to the leaves of the oak and beech, wondering if this acid was responsible for the unhappy, parched look to these new leaves. Certainly, the weather had not been the dampest of springs, but these leaves looked desperate for a drink of water, being dry and crinkly. Mary sympathised with the leaves, as she too often felt thirsty.

Having done the sheep field, Fido and Isaac inspected Bean, who was once again lying down, not following his mother.

On close inspection, Isaac could see a bald patch on his back that looked like a burn. Perhaps Bean would need some other medicine? Isaac thought that they had not yet attempted to address the lack of B12. He ought to start there.

Fido and Isaac returned for breakfast. Mary was busy sorting out the monthly tests of the water quality of the local streams. She was surprised to find that, even though there was plenty of foam, there were not enough ammonia or phosphates to show any pollution from the tests. She had seen the oily foam on the surface and wondered what it was and how the tests had not indicated pollution, in spite of the fact that there were negligible protozoa and invertebrates swimming around as they would have done normally.

Fido was choking and coughing again. Mary looked in his mouth. It was red, sore and his tongue was fissured. He appreciated being patted on his back whilst he brought up an enormous amount of sticky, foamy, white phlegm. John suggested he took Fido to the beach for some refreshing sea air. John was also keen to fly his kite over the smooth, clean air of the sea and sands, without the turbulence derived from over the rough, undulating land.

Mary was happy with the young chicks, who were tweeting excitedly as they had found the new food and fresh grass.

THE BROWNIAN MOTION

Now, Mary was testing numerous samples of the waters of local and distant fields for elemental sulphur. Certainly, the tests were cheaper, but surprisingly, the results were showing remarkably consistent findings. The sulphur was everywhere in the water, flowing in the ditch, brooks, streams and rivers to the sea. As Mary got her eye in, she could see it on the top of the water, like an oily layer that reflected the light like it was a mirror. Sometimes, the colours were split as if from a prism. There was always a lump of white foam in the eddy. Isaac started to question where the source of this element was from, thinking back to Fredrick's 'source – pathway – destination'. All the fields around were spread with the smelly black soup from the concrete abomasum, which digested the vegetable matter and food waste by a slow burn to produce, say, 40% carbon dioxide, 58% methane and 2% sulphur. Much of plant life is made up of sulphur, for instance in the proteins, helping to make longer chains, and it is also responsible for the rotting stinks coming from the essential greens like cabbages.

Isaac remembered that elemental sulphur was not soluble in water. The labs had found significant quantities of sulphur.

He could only imagine that sulphur was in tiny bits, not easily seen by the naked eye but easily incorporated into the soup. Time to get the microscope out of the cupboard!

Now, he could see small, white particles. These minute particles migrated to the edge of the water drop on the slide, luminescing on the side of the meniscus. Some were so small that in the sunlight, he could see them bouncing around in a completely random, independent fashion, as if they were alive. Mary, too, recognised this as Brownian motion, first described by Lucretius in 60BC in his book *De Rerum Natura*.

At that moment, John came in to say that Bean was walking more confidently since starting the B12 pills. Although, a couple of lambs were still limping and one of the sleepy ewes had difficulty breathing. Also, she was struggling trying to see with stinging, sticky eyes. On closer inspection, she could not swallow easily and could only drink water with difficulty. John continued with an observation that there were no shield bugs this year. Where had the great big cruiser bats – the size of crows, that used to fly high to the side of the wood down to the valley – gone? He had not seen them this year at dusk at all. Fido was feeling much better since his trip to the beach in the fresh air, where he had had to cough another dinner plate load of foamy, sparkly phlegm onto the sand. He could now breathe easier.

TITUS LUCRETIUS CARIS

While Fido and Isaac were checking the sheep, Mary was wondering where all this white dust was from. Of course, she knew that sulphur was normally yellow, maybe this was another variant. She thought back to the sulphur ponds and bubbling mud at Solfatara. Isaac, returning from the morning inspection, remembered well that biting battery acid smell of the sulphurous ponds resting in the brim of this old relict of a volcano. In Roman times, the area was referred to as 'the gates of hell' on the Phlegrean Fields. The gases from the underworld deposited as a yellow stain on the cooler rocks at the base of the caldera. The science of this phenomenon is explained by the phase diagram for sulphur. At some pressures and temperatures, the sulphur sublimes from solid to gas and then deposits back again without any intervening period of being in a liquid phase. This phenomenon is well written about and has been tested over time rather than by peer review. Now, Isaac was on his high horse as Mary was feeling tired and sleepy, wiping the windowsills down, trying to clean them of this ubiquitous hard, fine, sticky, insoluble dust. Mary started complaining about her cough and the stinging of her tongue again, suggesting that she was allergic to this dust. She had had many blood tests, including for allergies and aspergillus from the four large phials of blood collected by the doctor; none of them showed any positive results.

Mary was disappointed that she had not received any positive results and that Isaac's premonitions about the hormone weedkiller had turned out to be false leads. So, she looked at the original pictures of the camellia plants when they were first hit and discoloured. The tiny phone with which she had taken the pictures had a zoom facility that enlarged the photos. If they were taken correctly, in focus and while the camera was still, effectively, the magnification was as high as her (times thirty) hand lens. Those earlier photos taken months ago revealed the profusion of small, white dust particles on the leaves of the camellias, like those on the windowsills. From this promising start, she scoured the camera roll and, sure enough, the particles, small though they were, were everywhere and had left their mark on the affected leaves. Mary showed Isaac this new discovery. He thought that many of the plants photographed were not only covered in microscopic particles but were also suffering from particular diseases common to that species. He wondered whether the plants were ill primarily because of the effects of the dust. The diseases were therefore secondary to the dust.

Isaac cast his mind abroad. He knew that he should not believe everything reported in the newspapers, but there seemed to be an awful lot of fires blazing around the world. What if these flagrant countries had the same sulphureous dust on their leaves, and the leaves were dry; would that not explain their spontaneous combustion?

COMMUNICATION

Isaac was cogitating. Although he had missed *prima luce*, there was no need to check the sheep so early, as most ewes had lambed. Fido could still run round the sheep, whenever, telling them to gather up, ready for collecting them into the pens, where they could be worked on their feet, administered further vaccinations, lambs tagged, sprayed for fly treatment and then shorn. His strong eye was enough to bring the stupidest lamb to order. The older ewes understood this means of communication, it being well practised over the years and repeated many times; they knew where to go and not to defy Fido. However, they were far more interested in the smell of their food. Each plant had a particular scent that governed the ewe's reaction. Isaac thought it wonderful how the ewes could separate any individual blade they did not like by spitting it out of the side of their mouth whilst mashing the rest ready for swallowing. He wondered whether this was a confirmatory lesson to reject similar blades. Those succulent, tasty, soft leaves of the thistles were not protected by smell but by their sharp, painful spines on their prickles, a tangible message not to eat them. Other plants spread scent in the air to deter animals from eating them, like hemlock, smelling of old mouse. Some plants attract pollinators by the scent of their flowers, like borage.

The old flower meadows used to be a haven for insects attracted by the sweet, lazy, colourful smell drifting off the fields on a hot, humid summer's day. While in the full flow of this pungent dream, Mary came in remarking that, recently, she was unable to smell such loveliness, the perfume of nature, the hawthorn blossom, the old varieties of roses. Isaac thought back to Lucretius, noticing that those small particles of smell bouncing around in the air were now spreading the message at 30mph further afield. Isaac thought to himself: *Was that the speed of wind or would the particles be able to disperse in still air at that velocity?* At that time, Mary despaired that the trees were not coping when infected by a disease; normally, they would send out warning pheromones to other trees to say that they were being attacked. The healthy trees, smelling these attack hormones, would be vaccinated and therefore prepared to resist the new spreading virus or disease. Nowadays, it seemed the trees were unable to resist – could they not smell the danger as before in the past when they had shiny, dark green supple leaves?

Mary carried on dressing the first of three little young chickens, having killed them in the morning. As she tackled the insides, she noticed the gall bladder was unusually large, twice as big as normal, stretched like a balloon, full of dark green bile. Mary, although she had repeatedly complained that she could not smell anything, now had every reason to moan because these chickens had a more pronounced chickeny smell than normal, which tended to be unappetising.

BEAN'S DEMISE

Isaac was close to a dilemma. He hated having to make decisions like this one that would affect poor Bean's future. Although Bean's response to the various medicines had been good in the short term, once again Bean would rather sit in the field and do nothing. He was not particularly interested in number 138's milk; he was not ravenously hungry, which by now, at just over one month old, he should have been. He was not putting on weight; the vet did not know the cause of his affliction. Bean, although he had tried hard, might have to join Wheezer in the great field in the sky. Just as Isaac was thinking about this, he heard Mary ring the bell to summon him from the field to the telephone. Isaac thought that this was a bad omen for Bean because the bell may as well have been tolling for the calf. After Isaac had sorted the phone call, Mary showed him the outside of the brass bell. Isaac questioned Mary as to whether she had been polishing the bell outside with some modern chemical because it had become tinged with blue inside and out. She had relied on the natural patina and not attempted to add yet another job to her long list of housework ones. Isaac concluded that the blue colour must have been copper sulphate with which he treated the sheep's feet. The bell metal, brass, which he had bought from France, was traditionally made from 78% copper, 22% tin. Not surprisingly, the copper must have been attacked by sulphur in the air.

A similar train of events happened to the glass front of the wood burner. The glass door had cracked without any use; the fire had remained unlit for some time. Isaac had researched that this could happen when nickel inclusions in the heat-resistant glass were attacked by the sulphur in the air. As the fire had been dormant, the sulphur could have been sucked down the chimney by the cold, descending air. The thoughts of this cold downdraft spurred Isaac on to arrange for Bean to go to the Veterinary Authoritorium. Eventually, the results of his post-mortem came through. He had had a severe bacterial infection of his joints, basically joint ill, which explained his slow walk, coupled with marginal levels of selenium, usually responsible for white muscle disease, which might have accentuated this reluctance. Also, there with a ground, glass-like appearance to his spinal column. They also noticed the burn on his back. Isaac thought back – Bean had never breathed easily either.

In the past, Isaac and Mary had milked cows that did not have calves. It was an ideal way of discussing the plan for the day. Mary sat on her stool, milking her two teats on her side, with Isaac sitting on his stool opposite, milking his two teats on his side. Later on in the day, they would taste their rewards in the form of milk, yoghurt, cream, cheese and ice cream of many flavours. It was so delicious; the time doing this had always been well rewarded with that magical taste. No 138 was now full of milk and needed to be relieved. So, expectantly, they started milking her, then processing it. For such a big cow, she was not particularly generous in volume, but it looked so thick and creamy, just like the other cow's milk from previous farms. Later, Isaac and Mary were mystified when, even using the milk for tea, it tasted bitter, acid and rank. As for making cheese, it just would not 'go' properly. It did not fulfil the historic expectations from long ago. That milk was a great disappointment.

Maybe Bean had been right in the first place. He had had good cause not to relish it after all.

CHICKEN DRESSING

Isaac, Mary and John had thoroughly enjoyed the three little young poulets earlier. After the disappointment of 138's milk, they decided to revert to chicken for supper. The chickens in the roving pen were growing well. The system had always been very successful, producing tasty, clean chickens for roasting. Mary tackled just two larger specimens, half-grown to full size. She had killed countless numbers in the past. However, these two would not bleed properly. They seemed to have more blood than usual, which seemed to flood their necks and breast, leaving red bruises which were repeated on the ends of the wings. Later, she started on the vivisection; checking the livers for their health status, she noted that the gall bladder had only a yellow liquid inside with no green bile. As part of the investigation, she searched further to find a preponderance of blood vessels over the small intestine. Further up, and even on the breast, she could see more broken blood vessels with her hand lens bought originally for inspecting the lichens. Having prepared the chicken for supper, she was still puzzled that these two were like the last three: smellier and less appetising than normal. At supper, Isaac, brandishing the knife onto the steel, made a keen sharp edge. As he was about to carve, he noticed more chicken smell. The breast, though well cooked, showed brown flesh more like the leg meat. It was tasty, having been basted by the bacon rashers. The breast flesh was not as white as normal, showing some patches of browning. However, Mary preferred chicken because, lately, she had found that roast lamb gave her indigestion and stomach ache.

WHEATWORTHY

Mary was delighted with her surprise birthday present from Sophie. Her appreciative daughter had offered to pay for a short holiday at Wheatworthy. John was to be left at home in charge of the farm.

Unfortunately, Mary still had the VAT calculations to complete. She complained to Isaac that she just could not add up and that was the reason why they were delayed in departure. Isaac was somewhat grumpy as he had designed the spreadsheet to take the mental arithmetic out of the job. So, there should have been no problems with the calculations or even any necessity to do any. He had had to admire Mary's speed with a long column of numbers. In the past, when he had an error in the programming, she quickly located the faulty formula. Today, however, she seemed useless at sorting the VAT; she could not get her brain around the column of numbers! In fact, she was questioning herself and her ability to reason. It worried her.

Eventually, Isaac and Mary set off to a delightful, picturesque cottage in a quiet, secluded village the other end of Deltashire. On arrival, Isaac started exploring. He just happened across a local, who, by the untidy contents of his car – supers and frames at random – was obviously an apiarist, who spent his whole life looking after his hives of bees. Isaac had always marvelled at their hierarchy, particularly the life of the drone. All he had to do, having been totally pampered all his life, was fly off to meet the queens on the appropriate day. That day and place was known about by all the queens in the county. Each queen returned to their hives with fertilised eggs, ready to lay.

The local was distraught by the fact that none of his queens had returned from their nuptial flight. As an aside at about the same time, he had noticed a fine, thick white dust covering his old red car. His neighbour's cars suffered from this too, mind, theirs was less obvious, having been washed more frequently and recently. He offered Isaac a jar of honey as if to prove the bees' credentials, then dolefully wended his aching way, mumbling something about the local sewage works. *Was he aware that, nowadays, many of the sewage works had concrete abomasa to help deal with the waste?* questioned Isaac.

He returned to Mary in the cottage. He suggested that they could eat in the local pub. On the way, Mary inspected the hedges to find that, here too, there were plants blighted with the same orange/brown discoloured marks on their leaves. Some of the other plants were not true to their usual colours. Isaac was hungry; Mary was exhausted; they seemed to have been waiting all day; he keenly ordered their fare. Looking around, Isaac noticed a lady sat on a stool by the bar, coughing with that same note that Mary had had when she went to the hospitals and afterwards. The lady by the bar was debating what to order because, recently, she had lost her sense of taste and smell, making the choice provided by the comprehensive, varied menu difficult to resolve. Through a sympathetic conversation, she explained to them that, in spite of courses of antibiotics over several weeks, she was unable to shift her annoying cough. It remained with her to that day. Isaac and Mary promised to follow the saga next time they holidayed in Wheatworthy.

FOOD FOR FIDO

Mary was looking forward to picking the next chicken when they returned home. On the way back, they smelt the unmistakable organic chemical waft of a tanker with a chimney approaching before it had reached them. Isaac thought fondly of Lucretius. Mary wondered whether the bacteria within the soup were still alive and working to make the recognisable volatile organic chemicals like ether, mousy-smelling piperidine, phenols and cresols. She had asked the laboratory what other chemicals there might be in the black soup. They had suggested thiirane, a smelly, simple sulphur compound. Just after that suggestion, the Authoritorium, too, had decided to check for chemicals with diffusion tubes. Mary had read the instructions carefully for the siting and placement of the tubes; it said some with their caps on and for other chemicals, without caps at all. It was disappointing that the Authoritorium operatives did not seem to have a clue how and who should carry out the tests. Mary kept quiet, sure that this knowledge could be revisited at a later date, in case it all went legal.

After the long journey, Isaac thought he would have to wash the car because he had killed insects which, mixed with the dusty, white splashes smeared the windscreen. He set about washing the car windscreen and headlights. The glass was threatening to become smeary, nowhere near as bad as in former times when he had had to wash flies off the windscreen on each fill-up so that he could see, especially at dusk when travelling towards the west.

The chickens had grown well, motoring past their ugly and then their truculent teenager stages to become handsome, fully feathered adults. Mary chose the largest in the pen, missing out the croaky one, who always seemed to find himself in harm's way by being at the head of the queue just as Mary was bending down to grab the chosen one. Once again, Mary was disappointed that this chosen one would not bleed properly. After cutting his throat, it seemed as if he was still full of blood. She searched the insides to find that he had no bile at all! Nothing in the gall bladder – dry!

And now, that extra blood seemed to show as bruises all over the breast and wings. She took a closer look at the heart, which was larger than normal and was covered with swollen blood vessels. The small intestines seemed painfully inflamed, covered in many blood capillaries. The legs also showed larger blood vessels. Mary thought the carcass was not up to her exacting standards, so she sliced it up ready for Fido, marked it as such and put it in the freezer. Whilst washing up, Mary thought about her own varicose veins, which had ached so much recently. Also, her purple toes, though being quite colourful, occasionally tingled. Was this a symptom of too much blood in her relaxed veins?

Mary, on her visit to the supermarket, assessed the dressed chickens on display. They too, showed more visible blood vessels on the wings and breast of their carcasses. While in the market, she came across the local fishmonger, whose fish, especially the plaice, also suffered from extra prominent blood capillaries on the edges of the white flesh. Mary challenged him about these defects, to which he replied that, maybe, nowadays, the fish were being caught with less care.

PHASES

The Authoritorium decided, in response to repeated questions about the smells coming from the lagoon, to test around it. They put a special testing box by the site of the lagoon so that the instruments in the box could smell the lagoon contents. On account of testing for irrelevant chemicals, they found nothing of concern. The lagoon was filled by a vacuum tanker from the concrete abomasum on another site. The effluent, the black soup from the abomasum, was moved around the countryside by the vacuum tanker, relying on atmospheric pressure to push the soup from within the abomasum to fill the tanker. The space inside the tank welcomed the soup by sucking it in. Thus, the soup arrived in the tank under vacuum. Within the soup, there were many small grains of sulphur left over from the excreta of the bugs living in the concrete abomasum. These grains of sulphur were subjected to the vacuum too and were also nice and warm from the fermentations in the abomasum. The temperature was high enough and the pressure low enough, according to the phase diagram, for the sulphur particles to sublime into minute gas bubbles, small enough to be relatively stable in the soup into which they were insoluble, whether as solid or gas.

While the soup was being transported along the narrow roads of the countryside, although full, the tanker contents lurched on going round corners or while breaking and accelerating. This pushed waves and surges around the black soup so that some of the bubbles coalesced and then had enough buoyancy to escape up the chimney into the surrounding air of the hedges and trees on the roadside. These bubbles encountered higher pressure and lower temperature deposited into small solid particles of sulphur, slightly smaller, even, than the grains of sand blown from the Sahara. Not only was the sulphur affected by the vacuum, but also, the warm, volatile, organic compounds became more volatile and more mobile as the pressure was lowered by the vacuum. Mary listened carefully, if sceptically, to Isaac's explanation of the sulphur phases. Surely, with such small particles that were insoluble in water with nowhere to hide, they could just as easily bounce out of the black soup of their own accord? Anyway, what exactly were the temperatures and corresponding pressures in real life? Mary was keen to explain that when she was cooking, standing by the hot oven, she was aware of the fumes through feeling sick and drugged. She also noticed the tingly air on her tongue. She found similar effects from the computer cooling its microprocessor, blowing a draft of warm air. Maybe, that heat was causing the sulphur to follow the phase diagram. Isaac and Mary discussed these phase diagram revelations. The sulphur could be in either phase, solid or gas, as well as being invisible. The long list of sulphur effects could affect the plants, insects, birds, fish, animals (including humans); in fact, everything that is living on the planet. On that basis, Isaac and Mary, with John and Fido, decided to retire to a little remote croft on the west coast of Scotland, waiting for the Gulf Stream to revert back to its original course and strength.

POSTSCRIPT

Isaiah 34 KJV, possibly written circa three thousand years ago.

7 *And the unicorns shall come down with them and the bullocks with the bulls and their land shall be soaked with blood and their dust made fat with fatness.*

8 *For it is the day of the Lord's vengeance and the year of recompenses for the controversy of Zion.*

9 *And the streams thereof shall be turned into pitch* [hydrocarbons], *and the dust thereof into Brimstone* [sulphur] *and the land thereof shall become burning pitch.*

10 *It shall not be quenched night nor day, the smoke thereof shall go up for ever from generation to generation it shall lie waste, none shall pass through it for ever and ever.*